I1029522

HELLO KITTY®
and
♥ME♥

Hugs

Copyright © 2014 by Sanrio Co., Ltd.
Cover and internal design © 2014 by Sourcebooks, Inc.
Cover design by Randee Ladden and Brittany Vibbert
Text by Jacqueline A. Ball
Internal design by Tim Warren

Sourcebooks and the colophon are registered trademarks of Sourcebooks, Inc.

Published by Sourcebooks Jabberwocky, an imprint of Sourcebooks, Inc.
P.O. Box 4410, Naperville, Illinois 60567-4410
(630) 961-3900
Fax: (630) 961-2168
www.jabberwockykids.com

Library of Congress Cataloging-in-Publication data is on file with the publisher.

Source of Production: Worzalla, Stevens Point WI, USA
Date of Production: May 2014
Run Number: 5001672

Printed and bound in the United States of America.
WOZ 10 9 8 7 6 5 4 3 2 1

HELLO KITTY® and ♥ME♥

Hugs

Hello Kitty loves hugs. Hugs feel nice and tell others we care. Some hugs say hello.

Hello, Mama!

Some hugs
say thank you.
Thanks for the
tasty treat, Papa!

Hugs make us happy, especially on birthdays!

Some hugs say thanks, partner!

Some hugs
say good-bye.
Have a nice
vacation, Grandma
and Grandpa!

Hugs make us feel warm.

Hugs make us feel safe in a scary storm.

Hugs make us feel better.

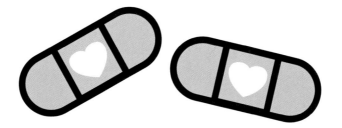

Hello Kitty always knows when someone needs a hug.

When a friend
tries hard...

...and things still go wrong...

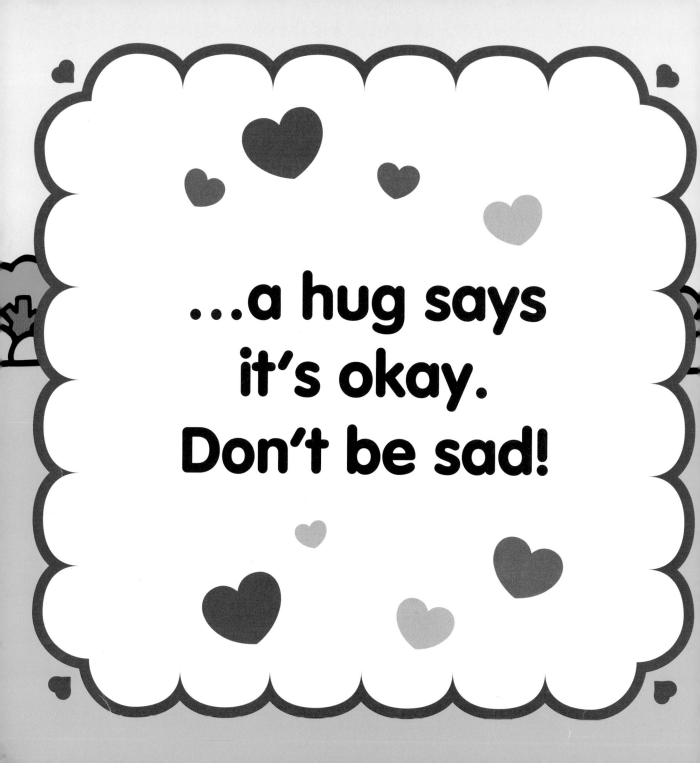

...a hug says
it's okay.
Don't be sad!

Hugs bring families together...

...and keep our friends close. You are Hello Kitty's friend, too!

A hug and a kiss say sweet dreams! Sleep tight!

Hugs come from our hearts. Here's a hug for you!

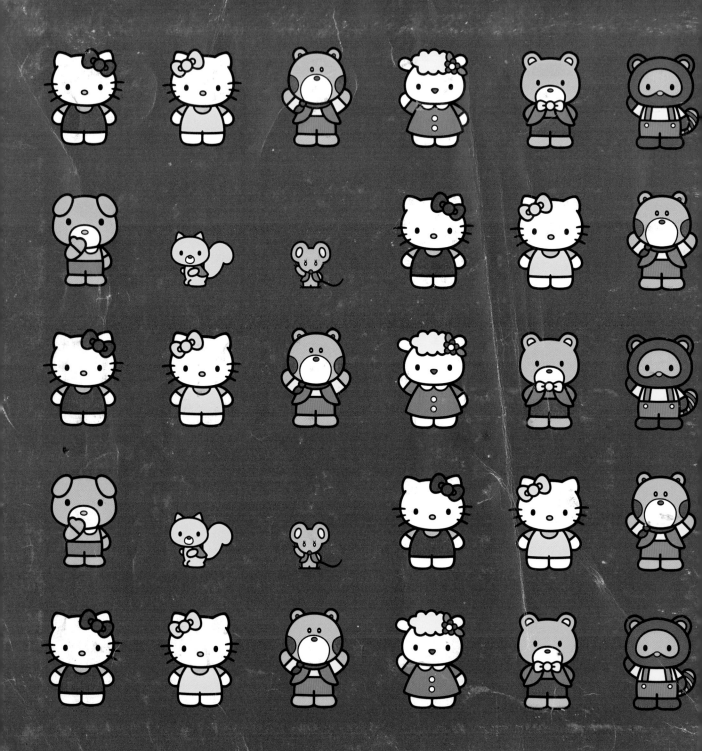